# LEGO Disney PRINCESS

# Enchanted Treasury

# Contents

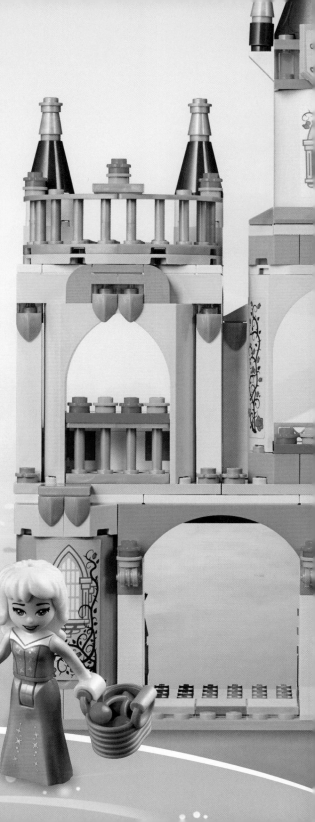

# Introduction

Welcome to the *magical* world of LEGO® *Disney Princess™*. Get ready to travel to *faraway lands* and learn the princesses' *fairytale* stories. Each princess faces different challenges on her *adventures*, but they have many things in common.

The princesses are *kind*, and *loyal* to their friends. They have the *courage* to stand up for what they believe in, even when faced with evil villains. They may live in *palaces*, but the princesses know that to be truly royal, it's what's in their *hearts* that counts.

# Cinderella

Hardworking and cheerful, *Cinderella* never stops believing things will get better, no matter how difficult life is. Despite being made to work as a scullery maid for her jealous stepmother, she is **kind** to all and dreams of a better life.

With a little help from her animal friends and her *Fairy Godmother*, Cinderella's *dreams* do come true!

# Working hard

Cinderella has to work hard in the kitchen.
All day long, she **cooks**, **cleans**, and **scrubs**.
Her stepmother and her stepsisters never lift a
finger to help. They make Cinderella do it all!

Cinderella cheers herself up by *singing* as she
sweeps the kitchen courtyard. But she cannot sing
for long. It's nearly time to serve breakfast,
and then there are the dishes to do.

*"There isn't any letup!"*

# Cinderella's friends

Cinderella loves her **animal friends**. They **encourage** her to hold on tight to her **dreams**. There is Major the horse, Bruno the dog, and Gus the mouse. Only one animal is unfriendly. That's Lucifer, her stepmother's sneaky black-and-white cat!

Something Cinderella loves to do is **make clothes** for her animal friends. She is so kind that she has even made a hat for naughty Lucifer!

*"We can help our Cinderelly!"*

# Prince Charming

There is to be a **ball** at the castle, and all the
young ladies in the land are invited. At the ball, they
will meet the **handsome** Prince Charming.
The King hopes that the Prince will fall in
love and start a family.

Prince Charming is not sure he is ready to marry, but
maybe he will change his mind. Cinderella's stepsisters
*can't wait* to meet him. Neither can Cinderella!

# Fairy Godmother

Cinderella's stepmother says Cinderella cannot go to the ball after all. She must stay home and do her chores. Poor Cinderella!

Then the Fairy Godmother appears, wearing a purple cloak. She tells Cinderella to dry her tears. She is going to work some *magic* ... if she can remember the spell! The Fairy Godmother is *forgetful* but kind. She may lose her wand, but she never loses her cheerful smile.

## "Bibbidi bobbidi boo!"

18

# Magical carriage

The Fairy Godmother has found her wand! She waves it, and a pumpkin turns into a **wonderful carriage**. She waves it again and turns Cinderella's mouse friend into a white horse.

The Fairy Godmother waves her wand a third time, and Cinderella's rags turn into a **ballgown** and **glass slippers**. Now Cinderella can go to the ball. But she must be careful to leave on time. The spell will be broken at the stroke of midnight!

*"Now, off you go!"*

20

# The glass slipper

At the ball, Prince Charming only has eyes for Cinderella. They **dance** all evening. But as the clock strikes midnight, she flees, leaving behind a glass slipper.

The Prince has fallen head over heels in love with the owner of the glass slipper. He **searches** the kingdom, asking every lady to try it on. It's a **perfect fit** for just one—Cinderella. Prince Charming asks her to become his Princess.

# Dream castle

The day of the **royal** wedding is bright and sunny. Three cheers for the Prince and Princess! After the ceremony, the happy couple return to their dream castle to **set up home**.

The castle has six **turrets** and flying flags. It has a throne room, a dressing area, a kitchen, a bedroom, and a dining hall. In fact, it has everything Cinderella and Prince Charming need to live **happily ever after**. And that's exactly what they do!

# Aurora

Kind and modest, *Aurora* was raised by her three *fairy aunts*. She only learned that she was a princess on her sixteenth birthday. Until then, she thought she was a peasant girl named *Briar Rose*.

Aurora has faith in the power of *dreams*. She learns that when *magic* and dreams combine, even the strongest of curses can be broken!

# Maleficent

**Wicked fairy** Maleficent is furious. She has not been invited to the party to celebrate Princess Aurora's birth! As revenge, Maleficent puts a *curse* on Aurora: on her sixteenth birthday, she will prick her finger and die.

Back in her *secret lair*, Maleficent settles into her black throne and cackles. Nobody insults her and gets away with it!

*"Stand back, you fools!"*

# Aurora in the forest

The **good fairies** hope to save Aurora from the curse. They rename her Briar Rose and hide her away in a cottage deep in the forest. Only on her sixteenth birthday will they tell her who she really is.

As she grows up, Aurora spends her days picking berries and singing to the **forest animals**. Then one day, a handsome stranger comes riding along. He looks just like a young man Aurora has met in her **dreams**!

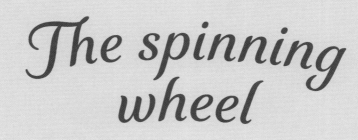

# The spinning wheel

It's the big day—Aurora's sixteenth **birthday**. At last, she learns she is a princess. The fairies take her to the royal **castle** for celebrations. Surely the danger from Maleficent's curse must be over now?

At the castle, Aurora is lured to a room with a **spinning wheel** in it. When she touches the spindle, she pricks her finger and falls into a **deep sleep**. The curse has worked, but only partly.

*"Sleeping Beauty, sleep on!"*

# The spell is broken!

Aurora continues *sleeping* in her four-poster
bed as Maleficent guards the castle.

Before long, someone bangs on the castle gate.
It is the handsome stranger Aurora met in the forest.
He's really a *prince*! Prince Phillip fights his way past
Maleficent and *wakes* Aurora with true love's kiss.
And with that, the curse is lifted forever!

# Ariel

The **merpeople** of Atlantica live under the sea.
Most of them are content with that, but not
*Princess Ariel*! She's simply fascinated
by the world above the waves.

Curious and bold, Ariel loves **exploring** shipwrecks
and **collecting** objects left behind by humans. She's
determined to follow her dream and venture into the
human world—whatever **risks** that might involve.

# Ariel's grotto

Ariel brings everything she finds back to her undersea *grotto*. She's got a ship's wheel, a treasure chest, and a mirror, among other things. Her fishy friend, *Flounder*, likes to explore her collection.

In her grotto, Ariel sings about the "gizmos" and "whatzits" she has collected. Where did they come from? Who owned them? She *imagines* what it might be like to live on land and walk on two legs.

## "It's just my collection!"

# Ariel's friends

Ariel shares all her secrets with her friends,
the **sea animals**. Although they love her dearly,
they wish she wasn't quite so headstrong. They want
her to be safe, as well as happy.

Flounder is Ariel's best friend. He is a timid little *fish*
but has a brave heart. Sebastian the *crab* writes songs
for Ariel and tries to keep her out of trouble. The little
*dolphin* gives Ariel rides. She holds onto his fin!

*"Life under the sea is better!"*

# Ursula's lair

The evil **sea witch**, Ursula, wants to become ruler of the sea. To do that, she will have to get rid of the rightful ruler. That's King Triton, Ariel's father.

Ursula is in her lair, her **tentacles** twitching with glee. She has a plan to gain **power** over King Triton. She will offer to help Ariel in exchange for her beautiful voice. The King will be devastated!

*"I fortunately know a little magic!"*

# Prince Eric

*Prince Eric* is looking for true love. He is sure he will know when he meets the right match. She will have to be **kind** and **sincere**, just like he is. Until then, the Prince spends his time happily **sailing** the ocean.

After a **shipwreck**, the Prince is rescued by Ariel. He wakes up to the sound of her beautiful voice singing to him. But she disappears into the ocean before he gets a look at her. Who could this enchanting creature be?

## "When I find her, I'll know!"

# A pact with Ursula

Ariel has fallen in love with Prince Eric.
Oh, if only she had legs instead of a **tail!** She could
go and live on land and find him again.

Ursula promises Ariel she can cast a spell to help.
There is just a small **price to pay**—Ariel's voice!
Ariel doesn't hesitate. She signs the contract and closes
her eyes. When she opens them, her voice is gone,
and so is her tail. Instead, she has human **legs!**

*"You can't get something for nothing, you know."*

# Magical kiss

Ursula has told Ariel she must get Prince Eric to **kiss** her within three days, or she will turn back into a **mermaid**. Then she will belong to Ursula!

Prince Eric does not know it was Ariel who saved him, but he begins to **fall in love** with her anyway. On a romantic boat trip, he is about to kiss her when their boat flips over. That night, Ursula wears a disguise and uses Ariel's captured voice to distract Eric.

*"Has he kissed her yet?"*

# Celebration time

Ariel's animal friends come to her *rescue*. They release her trapped voice and return it to her. Ursula is defeated, and Ariel tells Eric everything. Now for a wedding *celebration*—on the waves, of course!

The Celebration Boat is as *fancy* as can be. It has gold pillars, a dance floor, and even a place for Eric's dog, *Max*. As fireworks light up the sky, Ariel and Prince Eric sail off into a happy future together.

# Belle

*Belle* is the ***sweetest*** girl in her little town.
Local heartthrob Gaston wants to marry her, but
she would rather read ***books*** about faraway places.
The townspeople find that funny.

When Belle's father goes missing, she enters the woods
to look for him. She ends up in a place ***stranger*** than
anything in a book and learns that the most beautiful
thing of all is a ***kind heart***.

# Enchanted castle

When Belle's frail *father* goes missing in the *forest* on his way to an inventors' fair, Belle hurries to look for him. Oh dear ... this is not the adventure she wanted!

Belle finds that her father has been locked in an enchanted castle by an angry *Beast*! The castle is *beautiful*, with golden flags and gates, and a wonderful stained-glass window. How could it belong to someone so mean and horrible?

*"I'm looking for my father ..."*

# Belle's castle friends

Inside the Beast's castle, Belle meets the **magical servants**. They were once human, but an evil enchantress changed them into household objects.

Mrs. Potts the teapot and her playful son, Chip, make Belle feel at home. Lumiere the candelabrum and Cogsworth the clock soon become her **loyal friends**.

*"Be our guest!"*

# Belle's makeover

It's a good thing Belle likes the servants. She is going to be in the castle for a long time! She has agreed to stay as the Beast's **prisoner** in place of her father.

Wardrobe tries to cheer Belle up. She says the Beast isn't so bad, and Belle will live in **luxury** in the castle. She rummages through her drawers and picks out a **yellow gown** and gold tiara for Belle to wear to dinner with the Beast. Beautiful!

"*Let's see what I've got in my drawers.*"

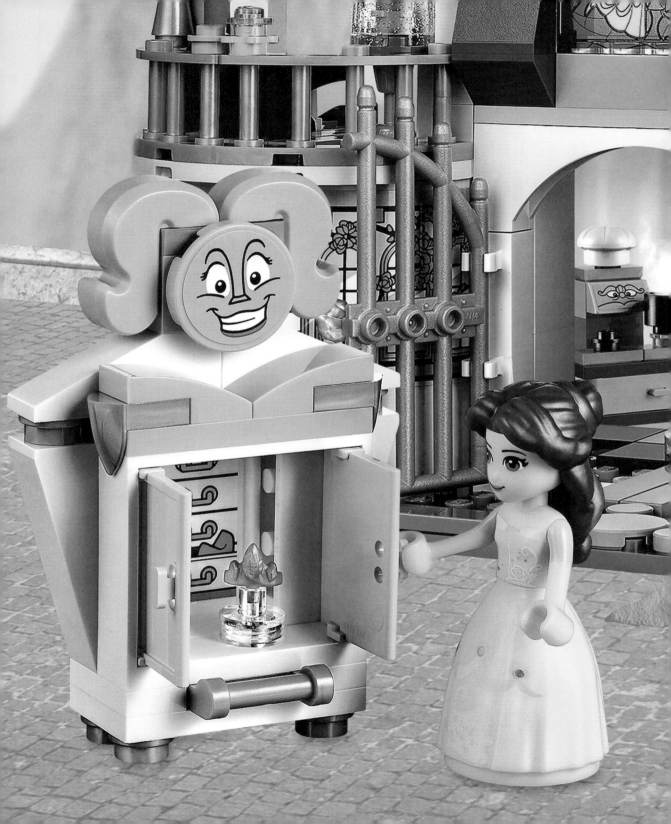

# The Beast

At first, Belle is scared of the Beast. Who wouldn't be? He has **sharp fangs**, horns, and a big shaggy mane. Belle doesn't know it, but he is really a prince who has been **enchanted**.

The Beast can't stand his appearance. It makes him **bad-tempered** because he thinks no one could love him. Only when he reveals his **gentle side** does he learn that friendships are built on kindness, not looks.

*"She'll never see me as anything but a monster!"*

# Magic mirror

The Beast becomes *fond* of Belle and does kind things for her. He even lets her have the castle library all to herself. Belle is very grateful, but nothing can stop her from missing her father, *Maurice.*

Belle pleads for a glimpse of her father through the Beast's *magic mirror*. But to her dismay, Maurice is very sick! The Beast cannot bear to see Belle so upset. He tells her she is free to *go home.*

*"Hold on, Papa. I'm on my way!"*

# Belle and the Beast

Once her father is out of danger, Belle races back to the castle. A **mob** of villagers are out to kill the Beast. Is she too late to stop them? It looks like the Beast has already been badly **wounded!**

Belle kneels and whispers "I love you." The Beast opens his eyes … then changes into a **handsome prince.** Belle's love has broken the **curse.** They celebrate with a romantic dance around the castle ballroom.

# Jasmine

Princess Jasmine is the **Sultan's daughter**.
She is by far the richest girl in the desert city of
**Agrabah**. Jasmine has everything she wants, from
gorgeous clothes and *jewels* to her own pet tiger.

A life of luxury makes some people lazy. Not Jasmine!
She is lively, curious, and very adventurous. Jasmine's
**independent** streak often leads her to clash with
her father, though she loves him dearly.

# Jasmine's palace

Princess Jasmine lives in a **splendid palace**, but she is unhappy. She is forbidden to leave the royal walls, and her father wants her to marry a royal prince.

Jasmine is **adventurous** and strong-willed. When she looks out from her balcony with her pet dove, she dreams of life beyond the palace.

## "If I do marry, I want it to be for love!"

# Aladdin

Aladdin is a poor **street urchin**. He has to steal food to survive, but he is not bad by nature. **Cheerful** and kind, Aladdin is happy to help anyone in need.

Aladdin is the only person allowed to enter the secret *Cave of Wonders*. He doesn't know this yet, but the Royal Vizier, Jafar, does! Jafar wants to force Aladdin to fetch him a **magic lamp** from the cave.

*"You're only in trouble if you get caught!"*

# At the market

Aladdin helps a young girl who has gotten into a bit of trouble with a merchant at the *market*. It's Jasmine! The daring Princess has sneaked over the palace wall to explore the outside world.

The new friends settle down to chat and nibble on some food (stolen, of course!). They learn that each has something the other dreams of. Jasmine has *wealth* and Aladdin has *freedom*. Yet neither is happy.

*"Sometimes you feel so ... trapped!"*

# Cave of Wonders

Aladdin agrees to enter the **cave** to look for the lamp. There it is, *glittering* in the darkness! But instead of taking it to Jafar, Aladdin rubs the lamp himself.

Whoosh! Out comes a *Genie*, who grants Aladdin three wishes. Aladdin's first wish is to become a *prince* so he can marry Jasmine. Later, he uses his second wish to escape Jafar and his third wish to set the Genie free from the lamp.

*"Genie, I wish for you to make me a prince!"*

# Magic carpet

Prince Ali is a **perfect match** for Jasmine. But she says no to marriage. She is in love with someone else … that ragged young man from the market, Aladdin!

Ali persuades Jasmine to ride with him on a magic **flying carpet**. As they swoop and soar around the world, Jasmine slowly recognizes Aladdin for who he is. In the end, even the Sultan has to agree that prince or **no prince**, Aladdin is the only one for Jasmine!

# Mulan

Mulan lives in Han Dynasty China. Strong-willed and *spirited*, she's always running into *trouble*. When her family takes her to see a local matchmaker, she accidentally spills tea everywhere!

Mulan longs to bring *honor* to her family. When her frail father is called to fight in the army, she takes his place to *save* him.

# Family ancestors

In Mulan's garden is a shrine in honor of her *ancestors*. Here, her family pray to the ancestors' spirits. They hope the ancestors will bring them *good luck*.

When Mulan sets off to join the army, the ancestors send a little Chinese *dragon* called Mushu to be her loyal *guardian*.

*"Ah, my ancestors sent a little lizard to help me?"*

# Brave warrior

Disguised as a man, Mulan **trains** hard in the army. She calls herself Ping. Her friends are her *loyal* horse Khan and Cri-kee, a lucky cricket.

Mulan has to prove to Li Shang, the army captain, that she's a good soldier. She is tough and *brave* and soon earns his *trust*.

# Making tea

When Mulan is revealed as a girl, she has to leave the army. Even so, her bravery and **quick thinking** save the Emperor and the Imperial city from the Hun army. The Emperor bows before Mulan—she is a **hero**!

Returning home, Mulan shares tea with her father. She has **brought honor** to her family at last, but they are just pleased to have her home!

# Snow White

Cheerful, *sweet-natured* Snow White is the fairest in the kingdom. This makes Snow White's stepmother, the Queen, jealous.

The mean Queen makes Snow White do housework all day long. But it doesn't get Snow White down! She's always singing *songs* and dreaming about a *happy* future.

# Snow White's friends

The Queen becomes so mean that she orders a Huntsman to take Snow White into the *forest* and kill her. But he can't bear to do it, and tells Snow White to run, run, *run*!

Deep in the forest, Snow White makes some friends. The *animals* are charmed by her *sweet voice*, and she is soon surrounded by friendly deer, squirrels, birds, and rabbits. Can they help her find a *new home*?

## "Maybe you know where I can stay?"

# In the cottage

The animals lead Snow White to a cozy woodland *cottage*. The furniture inside is tiny, and so are the cottage's residents … seven friendly *dwarfs*.

The dwarfs gladly let Snow White hide out there. To *thank* them, she helps around the cottage. While the dwarfs are at work in the mine, Snow White bakes them a gooseberry pie. Mmmm!

"Oh, it's adorable. Just like a doll's house!"

# An apple from a stranger

The Queen learns that Snow White is living in the woods. She disguises herself and takes an **apple** to the cottage. Snow White doesn't know that the apple is poisoned. She takes a bite and falls into a deep **sleep**.

The dwarfs are heartbroken. They keep watch over their sleeping friend. One day, a **prince** rides by and sees Snow White. He has been looking for her! His love breaks the evil spell, and Snow White **awakens**.

# Tiana

Everyone needs a dream! Tiana's dream is to open her own *restaurant* in New Orleans. It will be filled with good food, jazz music, and of course, happy customers.

This *ambitious* young woman doesn't waste time wishing she was rich, and she doesn't believe in magic. Wishes don't buy restaurants, and frogs don't turn into princes. It's *hard work* that makes dreams come true!

# In the café

What does Tiana mean by hard work? *Two jobs*, that's what! At night, she is a *waitress* at Cal's Diner, and by day, she works at Duke's Café.

Tiana has saved her *wages and tips*. She has nearly enough money to buy an old sugar mill that will make a perfect restaurant. Baking pastries in the café kitchen, she thinks about being her own *boss*. Not long now!

*"I'm gonna work a double shift tonight ..."*

# A magical adventure

Tiana is invited to her best friend's ball—but all she can think about is her restaurant. Out on the balcony, she finds herself next to a **talking frog**. Tiana doesn't know it, but the frog is actually the guest of honor, Prince Naveen, in disguise!

Tiana **kisses** the frog—and turns into a frog herself! It is the start of a magical **adventure** during which Tiana and Naveen fall in love. Working together, they break the spell cast on them and become human again.

# Tiana's Palace restaurant

Tiana and Prince Naveen are married in a royal **celebration**, with all their friends and family present. Now a **princess**, Tiana can finally open her restaurant, Tiana's Palace!

People come from everywhere to taste Tiana's cooking, especially her spicy **gumbo**. Her new husband provides some equally spicy **jazz** music. Tiana's Palace is definitely the hottest place in town!

# Rapunzel

Rapunzel has spent almost her whole life locked in a *tower*. That's nearly 18 years! No wonder she longs for an *adventure* outside.

She doesn't know it, but she is really a princess. As a baby, Rapunzel was *taken* by Mother Gothel, who knew a secret about Rapunzel's *long hair*. It has the *magical* power to keep Gothel young forever.

# Rapunzel's tower

Rapunzel has found many ways to **pass the time** in the tower. She reads, dances, knits, does pottery, and paints. *Brushing* her hair takes up plenty of time, too … about three hours a day!

When Mother Gothel visits, Rapunzel pulls her up to the ***tower window*** by her hair. She thinks Gothel is her real mother. Gothel is always warning Rapunzel about the dangers in the outside world.

# Keeping busy

There is always lots of housework to do. Rapunzel doesn't mind. It's another way of passing the time. Sweeping, polishing, and dusting are not very exciting, but **baking** can be fun.

Rapunzel's only friend is her pet chameleon, *Pascal*. He's always trying to coax Rapunzel to escape outside to play. He cannot speak, so he points with his tail!

*"Oh, come on Pascal... it's not so bad!"*

# Flynn

*Flynn Rider* began life as a poor orphan. As he grew up, he took to stealing. Flynn hides his **kind** and gentle side under a **charming** and vain exterior.

It's Flynn's ambition to own a **castle** one day. He is planning a big scheme at the **palace**, so perhaps he will be able to buy one if he gets away with it!

*"Can't you picture me in a castle of my own?"*

# Rapunzel and Flynn

Flynn surprises Rapunzel when he climbs the tower to hide out after stealing a **crown** from the palace. She surprises him by hitting him with a **frying pan**!

Rapunzel begs Flynn to take her to see some floating **lanterns** that appear in the sky once a year. The King and Queen release them to mark their lost daughter's **birthday**. Rapunzel doesn't know that's her!

"Fine, I'll take you to see the lanterns."

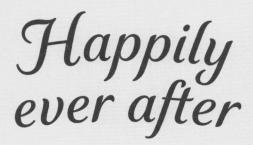

# Happily ever after

The kingdom of **Corona** seems oddly familiar to Rapunzel. She realizes she has been here before.

Flynn has fallen *in love* with Rapunzel. He wants Mother Gothel to leave her alone, so he *cuts off* Rapunzel's magical hair. Gothel shrivels into dust! Now the happy couple can be together always, and Princess Rapunzel can take her place in the *royal family*!

# Moana

Moana is the **chief's daughter**, and they live on the island of Motunui. One day, she will be leader and she will do things her way. Moana is very **strong-willed**!

All her life, Moana has longed to explore the **sea**. But her father has banned anyone from sailing beyond the **reef**. Moana learns that sometimes the **courage** to disobey can be the greatest courage of all.

# Moana's island

The island of *Motunui* is a lush world of pale sands and coconut palms, but lately something is wrong. A mysterious *darkness* has taken over the land. The plants are dying, and there are no fish in the sea.

In a secret cave, Moana sees a vision of her *ancestors* … sailing! They had to stop sailing after someone stole the heart of the goddess *Te Fiti*. If Moana can return the heart, will the darkness disappear?

## "We were voyagers!"

# Moana's friends

It was *Maui* who stole the heart of Te Fiti! This ancient demigod can turn into all kinds of animals. He carries a magic **hook** and is covered in **tattoos**. Moana will need his help to return the heart.

Moana's animal friends help her, too. There's Pua, her *pig*, and Heihei, her **rooster**. On her adventure, she meets turtles and a manta ray that is really the spirit of her dear *grandmother*.

*"Maui always has time for his fans!"*

# Ocean adventures

Persuading Maui to help is tricky, but worse is to come. Moana and her friends face **ocean storms**, pirates, a giant crab, and a lava monster before they can even get close to Te Fiti.

Moana's **canoe** takes quite a beating! Along the way, she learns lots of sailing skills from Maui, such as **navigating** by the **stars**. Moana becomes a wayfinder—an expert sailor.

"We can find a way around!"

# Welcome home!

Once Te Fiti has her heart back, the darkness lifts. Moana hugs Maui goodbye and sails home to Motunui in *triumph*. Plants are growing and fish have returned to the water!

The *villagers* come running. Hooray for Moana! Moana briefly relaxes in her island house. Tomorrow, she will begin teaching her people to sail so they can all be *voyagers* once again, like their ancestors.

**Senior Editor** Laura Palosuo
**Art Editor** Elena Jarmoskaite
**Production Editor** Siu Chan
**Production Controller** Lloyd Robertson
**Managing Editor** Paula Regan
**Managing Art Editor** Jo Connor
**Art Director** Lisa Lanzarini
**Publisher** Julie Ferris
**Publishing Director** Mark Searle

**Written by** Julia March

DK would like to thank Randi Sørensen, Heidi K. Jensen, Paul Hansford, and Martin Leighton Lindhardt at the LEGO Group and Chelsea Alon at Disney. Thank you to Rachael Parfitt for the cover border illustration, Gary Ombler for additional photography, and Kayla Dugger for proofreading.

First American Edition, 2020
Published in the United States by DK Publishing
1450 Broadway, Suite 801,
New York, New York 10018

A catalog record for this book
is available from the Library of Congress.
ISBN: 978-1-4654-9788-8
978-0-7440-2372-5 (Library Edition)

DK books are available at special discounts when purchased in bulk for sales promotions, premiums, fund-raising, or educational use. For details, contact: DK Publishing Special Markets, 1450 Broadway, Suite 801, New York, New York 10018. SpecialSales@dk.com
Printed and bound in China

For the curious
**www.dk.com**